Handa

Grandma

Akeyo

Mondi

The big, bad goat

WHERE'S MONDI?

"**W**here are you?" said Handa.
"Mondi! Mondi!"

Grandma had a black chicken called
Mondi. Every day, Handa gave Mondi
her breakfast. But one day, she didn't
come.

"Grandma, have you seen Mondi?"
said Handa.

7

"No," said Grandma. "But I can see your friend!"

"Akeyo!" said Handa. "Help me find Mondi."

The two friends looked all around
the chicken-house. *Cluck ... cluck.*
They saw brown hens and white
hens and —

"Look!" said Akeyo.
Flap ... flap.

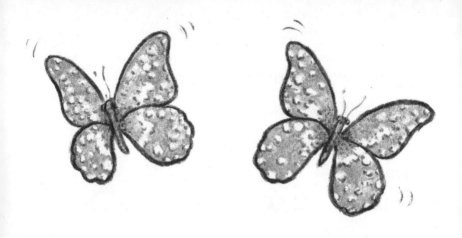

Two big spotty butterflies flew past. "Very pretty," said Handa. "But they're not Mondi. Maybe she's under the grain store."

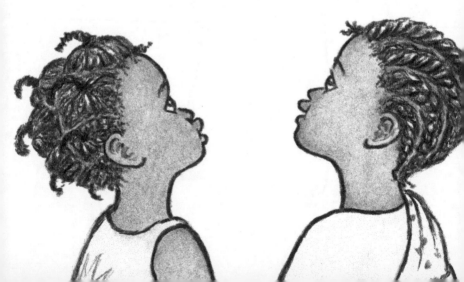

They peeped under the grain store.
Squeak ... squeak. Three tiny
mice were nibbling grains of
sweetcorn. They ran when
they saw the girls.

"Mondi's not here," said
Handa. "Let's see if she's
behind those pots."

They peeped behind some big, red
pots and found …

Pit-a-pat … pit-a-pat.

"Lizards!" said Akeyo.

Four little yellow and blue
lizards were running in and out
of the pots.

"But where's Mondi?"
said Handa.

"She might
be hiding in
those trees,"
said Akeyo.

The trees were full of red flowers.
Sip ... sip. Five green and orange
sunbirds were sipping juice from
the flowers.

"I can't see Mondi," said Handa.

14

"Maybe she's gone up the hill."
They climbed up to the top.

"Look!" said Akeyo. *Hop ... hop.*
Six jumpy crickets were hopping in
the grass.

"I want to catch them!" said Akeyo.

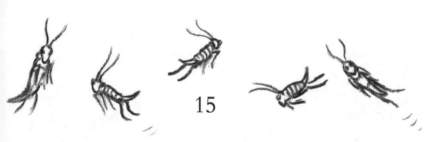

"I want to find Mondi,"
said Handa. "Let's go
down to the waterhole.
She may have gone
for a drink."

The waterhole
was as big as a lake.

"Look! Down there!"
said Akeyo.

Croak ... croak.

Seven baby bullfrogs
with big, round eyes
were catching flies.

"But where's... Oh!
What's this?" said
Handa. "Footprints!"

The girls followed
the footprints.
Slurp ... slurp.

"Oh, no. Spoonbills," said Handa. There were eight big birds with bills like spoons. They were slurping water from the lake.

"Mondi's really gone," said Handa.

"Maybe a spoonbill ate her," said Akeyo. "Or maybe a *lion* gobbled her up!"

Handa felt sad. They walked back towards Grandma's.

"Look there!" said Akeyo.

Peck … peck.

Nine cheeky starlings were
stealing sweetcorn from a field.
Handa wasn't looking.
"Listen," she said.
Cheep ... cheep.
"What's that?"

Cheep … cheep.
"It's coming from under
that bush. Shall we peep?"

Handa and Akeyo bent down
to look. It was dark under the bush.
They could see broken eggshells.
Something was moving.

Cheep … cheep.

"Chicks!" said Akeyo.

Cluck ... cluck.

"Mondi!" said Handa.

Mondi came out into the sunshine with ten fluffy chicks. They were black, brown, yellow and white. "Wow!" said Handa and Akeyo.

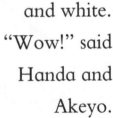

They ran back to Grandma's as fast
as they could.

"Clever Mondi!" said Grandma.
"Now come and have some breakfast."

Mondi and her chicks
had sweetcorn
and water.
The girls had
corn bread and
cool, fresh milk.

"What a surprising morning!" said
Handa.

"I love surprises," said Akeyo. She
got up to go back to her village. "Bye!"

"See you later," said Handa.

"There may be more
surprises today!"

THE FRUITY SURPRISE

tangerines

banana

guava

orange

mango

pineapple

passion-fruit

avocado-pear

"I can't wait to give Akeyo this surprise," said Handa. She put seven tasty fruits in a basket: a yellow **banana**; a sweet **guava**; a juicy **orange**; a red **mango**; a big **pineapple**; a green **avocado-pear**; and a purple **passion-fruit**.

"I wonder which fruit my friend will like best?"

Handa balanced
the big, round basket on top
of her head. She stood up slowly
and set off for Akeyo's village. She
could see the dry, dusty path. But she
couldn't see anything above her head.

28

So Handa didn't
see something with
hairy arms and
a long tail.
It was looking
down from a
tree at her fruit.

A monkey!

"I bet Akeyo likes the **banana** best," said Handa. The monkey swung down and grabbed … the banana!

Handa didn't see it had gone. She just walked happily on.

30

Something was hiding in the tall grass
by the path. It had a long neck
and a pink beak. It spotted
Handa's fruit.

An ostrich!

"Akeyo's best fruit may
be **guava**," said Handa.
The ostrich tiptoed up
behind her and
gobbled … her guava!
Handa didn't see a
thing. The sun was
hot, but a breeze
kept Handa cool.

Something else was hiding in the long grass. Something with black and white stripes. It could smell her lovely fruit.

A zebra!

Will the **orange** be
Akeyo's favourite?
thought Handa.

The zebra peeped
out and snatched …
the orange! Handa
heard the grass
shake behind her.
"It must be the
wind," she said.

34

Soon Handa was
half-way to Akeyo's.

Something
moved in the
grass behind her.
It had great
big flappy ears …
and a trunk. It had
seen Handa's fruit.

35

An elephant!

"Maybe the **mango** is
Akeyo's favourite," said Handa.
The elephant put out its trunk
and took … Handa's mango!
The basket wobbled.

"Oops!" said Handa.
"That wind is strong."
She walked on. The grass by
the path was tall, like a wall.
Handa didn't see the
tallest animal in the
world. It was looking
down at her fruit.

A giraffe!

Handa wondered if
Akeyo would like the
pineapple best.

The giraffe bent down. It lifted up …
her pineapple! The basket rocked.
"Help!" said Handa. "My basket
feels lighter but I'm too scared to
look round. Is there a monster?"
Handa walked faster. Something
with long, twisty horns
was peeping through
the grass. It saw
Handa's fruit.

An antelope!

"I'll soon be there,"
said Handa. "I wonder if
Akeyo will like the **avocado** best?"
    The antelope crept up
and stole ... the avocado!
    Handa didn't see. She hurried on,
past fields and trees.

40

Something was
sitting on a branch
above her head.
It had red and
green feathers
and a sharp beak.
It spotted Handa's
last fruit.

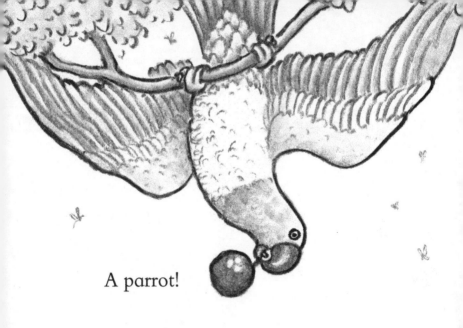

A parrot!

"Nearly at Akeyo's," said Handa. "Will she like the **passion-fruit** best?"

The parrot picked up … the passion-fruit! Now Handa's basket was *empty*.

Something else was looking at Handa. It had horns, and a rope around its neck.

"Akeyo's big, bad goat!" said Handa, walking past. "I'm glad it's tied to a post." The goat pulled the rope. Oh, no! The rope broke.

The goat charged after Handa. *Da dum, da dum,* **da dum**...

But it tripped on the rope and crashed into a fruit tree, just as Handa went under it.

Little orange fruits fell, *pit-a-pat, pit-a-pat*, into Handa's basket. Handa walked into the village.

"Akeyo!"
she called.
"I've brought you
a surprise."
"Tangerines!"
said Akeyo.
"My favourite fruit."
"Tangerines?" said Handa.
"That *is* a surprise!"

They lifted the basket down. It was
filled with sweet tangerines.

"Let's have a picnic!" said Akeyo.
All their friends had a wonderful time,
peeling and eating the juicy little fruits.

THE BIG, BAD GOAT

"What a lovely day I've had at Akeyo's," said Handa. On the way to her friend's village, Handa had lost seven fruits. But she had *found* lots of juicy tangerines. They'd had a tangerine party!

Now Handa was on her way home.

She had ten tangerines in a basket
on her head. A present for Grandma.

"What happened to my seven fruits?"
Handa wondered.

"A passion-fruit, an avocado-pear,

a pineapple, a mango, an orange,

a guava and a banana?"

50

Akeyo's big, bad goat was looking
at Handa. It shook its long horns and
the rope around its neck. It wanted to
butt Handa – to hit her with its head.

Handa spotted
something small and
purple on the dusty
red path.

"A passion-fruit
skin! That's odd,"
said Handa. "I lost
a passion-fruit
this morning."

The goat charged at Handa.
*Da dum, da dum, **da dum**...*
But it didn't come near. Its rope
got stuck between some rocks
and the goat was pulled off
its feet. *Urrrk!*

Handa didn't see
the goat, but she
saw something green
and shiny on the
ground. A squashed
avocado-pear.

"My goodness!" said Handa as she walked past. "I lost an avocado this morning." The goat pulled its rope free. Cross and dusty, it ran to butt Handa. *Da dum, da dum,* **da dum**...

But it skidded on the squashed avocado – *Wheee!* – and landed in a prickly bush.

Handa was way in front now.
She saw a large yellow "lump" poking
out of the grass by the path.

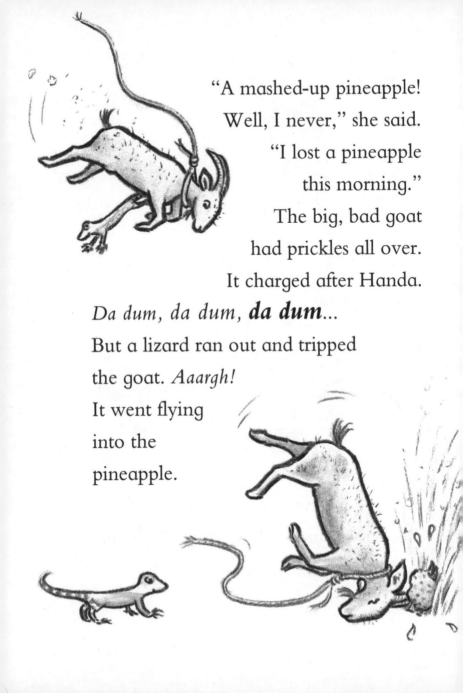

"A mashed-up pineapple!
Well, I never," she said.
"I lost a pineapple
this morning."
The big, bad goat
had prickles all over.
It charged after Handa.
Da dum, da dum, **da dum**...
But a lizard ran out and tripped
the goat. *Aaargh!*
It went flying
into the
pineapple.

Handa was half-way home now.
She saw a creamy-white stone on the
path, by some very tall grass.

"A mango stone! Well, well," said Handa. "I lost a mango this morning."

The goat had the pineapple stuck on its horns. It charged. *Da dum, da dum,* **da dum**...

But an elephant's baby peeped out of the grass.

It pulled the goat's tail – *Ouch!* – and ran back to its mum.

Handa held her basket of ten tangerines as she passed a big hole in the path.

She spotted something orange next to the hole.

"Orange peel! Fancy that,"
said Handa. "I lost
an orange this
morning."

The goat had
a very sore tail,
and pineapple juice
in its eyes. It charged again.
Da dum, da dum, **da dum**...
It fell in the hole,
head-first. *Plunk!*
Its legs waved
in the air.

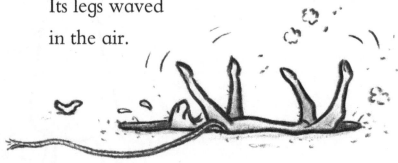

"I'll soon be home,"
said Handa. "Grandma
will love these
tangerines."

She saw a pale green
leaf on the path,
and something
yellowy-brown
under a tree.

"That looks like
a guava leaf – and
a banana skin! How
funny," said Handa.
"I lost a guava *and*
a banana this morning."

The big, bad goat
came out of the hole
with a lump on its
head. It was mad and it
badly wanted to butt Handa.

Da dum,
da dum,
da dum...

Handa didn't
see the goat and she
couldn't see the
monkey in the tree.

The monkey
was throwing
the tangerines
– *Ouch!* –
at the goat.

Ouch!
Ouch! Ouch!
A tangerine hit
the goat's bottom.
Ouch! It went
running back to
Akeyo's village.

Handa didn't see a thing. She walked on to Grandma's house.

"Grandma! Ten tangerines!" said Handa.

Grandma gave her a big hug. Then Handa looked in her basket.

"*Five* tangerines? But I set off with ten. What a surprising day!"